This Book Belongs to:

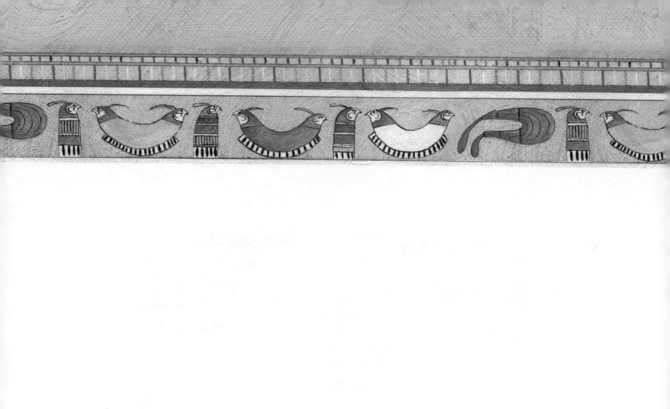

Miu and the Pharoah

ISBN 10-digit: 1 84401 872 5
ISBN 13-digit: 978 1 84401 872 7

First Published 2007
ATHENA PRESS
Queen's House, 2 Holly Road
Twickenham TW1 4EG
United Kingdom

Printed for Athena Press

Miu and the Pharaoh

Sally Wallace-Jones

Illustrated by
Robert Reader and Ally Gore

ATHENA PRESS
LONDON

*For John, with love
and in memory of my parents, who loved Egypt.*

Thousands of years ago, a small black cat called Miu lived in Egypt in the garden of a powerful Pharaoh. Miu was quite small, with soft black fur, glittering green eyes and a black button nose.

He was very slim, but his ears were huge. When he worried about it, his mother always reassured him and said that he would grow into them.

'Large ears are a sign of nobility,' she told him.

In the centre of the Pharaoh's garden, there was a pool filled with sparkling water and lotus flowers. Around this pool grew clumps of papyrus, shady palms, cornflowers, poppies, and bushes with brightly coloured flowers.

Miu's favourite game was to pat these flowers about when they fell to the ground. He could play wherever he wanted in the garden, but he was not allowed to go into the palace; and of course, that was exactly what he wanted most – to be allowed inside as a palace cat.

One day, Miu was dozing in the shade of a large bush, when he was suddenly awoken by a loud noise. He could hear lutes and pipes and trilling flutes – the music was so beautiful that he knew the Pharaoh must be nearby. Then a fragrant perfume wafted towards him. Next, a large pair of feet stopped right by the bush.

Miu gulped. The feet were wearing beautiful golden sandals, and he knew that they could only belong to the Pharaoh.

Miu took a deep breath and looked up. He could see at
once that the Pharaoh looked very unhappy. He seemed
not to notice the music, didn't speak to his courtiers and he
hardly admired the beautiful flowers either. Miu wanted to
go and rub himself around the Pharaoh's legs but he felt too
scared, so he stayed hidden in the bush.

Then suddenly a terrible thing happened. A flower fell off a tree and plopped down on the ground right next to where Miu was hiding. Before he knew what he was doing, Miu had jumped out of his bush and pounced on the flower. Just as he jumped out, the Pharaoh took a step forward and…

CRASH!

He fell right over Miu!

There was an awful silence. Miu crouched in the dust, terrified of what would happen next. The Pharaoh stood up slowly. He was streaked with dust and dirt and he didn't look very dignified at all.

Miu whimpered with fear. What would happen now? Perhaps he would have to leave the beautiful palace garden and live in a dark alleyway.

Then a pair of very strong but surprisingly gentle hands lifted him up.

'And what have we here?' asked the Pharaoh, looking right into Miu's terrified eyes.

'Only a cat, Your Majesty,' muttered a servant. 'Shall I have it removed?'

Miu held his breath, but the Pharaoh's voice was gentle as he replied, 'No. He meant no harm.' The Pharaoh smiled at Miu. 'It was a silly accident wasn't it, little friend?'

Then he asked, 'And who are you?'

'I'm a palace garden cat; my name is Miu,' came the brave reply.

The Pharaoh laughed.

'Greetings, Miu,' he replied. He stroked Miu's head and exclaimed, 'What big ears you have!'

'My mother says I'm going to grow into them,' Miu retorted, 'and that they are a sign of nobility.'

Then he added, 'Are you going to grow into your ears too?'

All of the courtiers gasped. Just like Miu, the Pharaoh had very large ears. In fact, it was embarrassment about his large ears that made him so miserable. Of course, no one dared mention the Pharaoh's ears in public! Miu knew he had said something he shouldn't have. He was too afraid to move.

Suddenly the Pharaoh gave a bellow of laughter. He laughed and he laughed and he laughed. Soon everyone was laughing and even Miu felt happy enough to start purring again.

'Thank you, little friend,' said the Pharaoh. 'Until today, I have felt embarrassed by my ears, but from now on I shall remember that I am growing into them.' And he added gravely but with his eyes twinkling, 'They are indeed a sign of nobility. Miu, I would like you to come and live in the palace and remind me to be proud of my ears. You can help me to remember that what matters is what I am like inside instead of worrying about how I look outside.'

Miu was speechless. At last, he would be a palace cat.

'Yes please,' he purred.

'Then we shall expect you this evening,' said the Pharaoh.

Miu had only ever seen the palace from a distance, and when he drew near it, it seemed much bigger than he had expected. He felt very small. The mud bricks were painted brilliant white and he was dazzled by the beauty of the palace in the rosy evening sun.

At the door, a smiling man introduced himself as Nakht Ankh, the Pharaoh's adviser. Miu trotted happily into the palace behind Nakht Ankh with his tail up. As soon as he stepped inside, he felt that he was in a magical new world. The rooms were enormous. The walls, floors and ceilings were all decorated with glowing colours and beautiful patterns. One room was covered from top to bottom with deep blue-green tiles. They fitted together so perfectly that all the walls seemed to shimmer with pools of light.

Eventually, Nakht Ankh stopped and said, 'This is the palace office, Miu. Please wait, while I find the Pharaoh.'

Nakht Ankh bowed and left. Soon Miu began to feel hot, bored and restless. He jumped off the chair and began to explore the room. Lining the walls were chests containing hundreds of rolled up papyrus scrolls. Miu listened carefully – he was sure he could hear a rustling noise inside one of them. Could it be a mouse?

He jumped into the chest, determined to catch it, and knocked all of the scrolls on to the marble floor. Miu discovered, to his delight, that papyrus scrolls were bouncy and springy and even better to play with than flowers.

Soon the scrolls were quite flat and much less fun to play with, so he climbed into another chest and bounced some more.

It was very dusty and soon Miu's fur was grey. He was also very thirsty.

Where can I find some water? he wondered. He crept over to the open door and gave it a push.

The floor outside was beautiful, shiny pink granite. Miu began to play – then he had a surprise which stopped him in his tracks. He skidded to a standstill in front of a statue of the cat goddess Bastet!

The goddess seemed to be looking at him rather disapprovingly. Miu bowed his head respectfully to the powerful, wise mother of all cats and asked for her blessing.

At the end of the corridor was another door. Miu slipped through it, and found himself in a magnificent bedchamber. There was a splendid bed, piled high with cushions. He was in the Queen's bedchamber!

On one side of the bed was a reed screen, concealing a marble bath that was sunk into the floor, and on the other was the Queen's dressing table, with lots of interesting jars on it.

Miu jumped on to the bed and began testing the cushions for comfort and kneading his paws into the soft mattress. Then he climbed up the screen.

Up and up he went, paw over paw, like a monkey climbing a palm tree. Then he launched himself off on to the cushions below. He was having such fun!

After a while, he looked around for something a bit less energetic. He sprang on to the Queen's dressing table and sniffed delicately at all the different pots and jars. Some of the pots smelt lovely, but one of them was full of powdery stuff that made him sneeze again.

He quickly moved on. There was a large, ebony box standing open, and when he looked inside it he could hardly believe his eyes. It was filled to the brim with precious stones and gold. These must be the Queen's jewels!

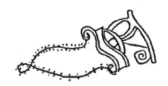

Miu could see rings, necklaces, bracelets and anklets made of gold and precious stones. The rich colours – dark blue, turquoise, purple, red and green – fascinated him. There were flowered hairpins and several large, square necklaces inlaid with figures and patterns. The Queen also owned a magnificent collar made from many strands of beads. Another necklace had great golden lion heads set between amethyst beads.

Then Miu saw something very strange. It had a slim, black handle inlaid with gold and precious stones. Above the handle gleamed the golden face of the cow-eared goddess Hathor. She supported a disc of shiny silver, but when Miu looked at the disc another cat smiled back at him!

Miu leapt back in shock and then laughed as he realised that it was his own reflection in the Queen's mirror!

As he jumped back, he caught one of the dark stone pots and it fell over, spilling scented oil across the floor. But that was not all; something hard and shiny also fell out and rolled on to the floor with a clatter.

Miu chased after it. He tried to catch the object but every time he tapped it with his paw it rolled away from him. He stopped to catch his breath and looked carefully at what he was playing with. It was a small, tapered cylinder, about as long as one of his whiskers, with a loop at the narrower end. It gleamed a dull yellow; could it be gold?

Miu held it still with a firm paw and licked it. A pattern of triangles began to appear. Some gleamed smoothly and others, made from hundreds of tiny golden beads, had a sparkly, rough surface. It was the most beautiful object Miu had ever seen. But he didn't have long to admire it, for just then the door opened and one of the Queen's maidservants appeared. When she saw the bedchamber she screamed.

'Look at this mess!' she exclaimed. 'Did you do all this?'

Miu hung his head. The maidservant glared at him, then she noticed the cylinder.

'Why,' she exclaimed, 'that's the Queen's missing necklace! She's been frantic trying to find it. She'll be delighted. The necklace was a special gift from Pharaoh; it is unique and very precious. I'm sure you'll get a reward.'

Miu purred with relief and they began to tidy up.

The room was just beginning to look neat when they heard shouting in the corridor and a very angry Nakht Ankh appeared. He spotted Miu and began to shout again.

'Was it you that made such a mess in the office?' he yelled. 'I've a good mind to throw you out of the palace, you little scallywag!'

The maid quickly stepped in front of Nakht Ankh holding up the necklace.

'Don't be angry with Miu,' she said. 'I'm sure he'll help to clear up, and just look! He's found the Queen's special necklace. I know the Queen and Pharaoh will forgive him when they see it.'

Nakht Ankh still looked grumpy but he agreed that Miu had done well to find the necklace.

'We'd better go and see the Pharaoh to tell him what's happened,' he said.

They set off through the palace until they came to a magnificent huge, hall. The high ceiling was supported by a forest of columns arranged in rows and carved to look like lotus flowers in bud.

The walls and columns were decorated with the Pharaoh's names and his many royal titles. Miu felt tiny and overawed as they walked the length of the room in the light from the high, latticed windows.

At the far end of the room was a raised dais where the Queen and the Pharaoh were sitting. Miu, Nakht Ankh and the maid bowed. Nakht Ankh began to explain about the mess in the office. When he had finished the Pharaoh looked very stern. Then the Queen's maidservant stepped forward.

'Please, Your Majesty,' she began, 'I know that Miu has been naughty but he helped to clear up, and look! He's found your lost necklace.' The maid presented the beautiful golden cylinder. There were tears in the Queen's eyes and she bent to stroke Miu's head.

'Thank you,' she whispered. The Pharaoh smiled.

'Just tell me one thing, Miu,' the Pharaoh asked gravely, 'why did you make such a mess in the office?'

'I thought I heard a mouse,' Miu explained. 'I wanted to stop it chewing your documents. I just got a bit carried away'.

'I see,' said the Pharaoh, his eyes twinkling.

The Queen rose and whispered in the Pharaoh's ear. The Pharaoh smiled. He spoke briefly to Nakht Ankh, then he turned to Miu.

'Miu,' announced the Pharaoh, 'in recognition of your help today we hereby appoint you Son of Bastet, Keeper of the Ears and Overseer of the Palace Mice.'

The Queen came forward holding a beautiful golden collar.

'All courtiers must wear a golden collar,' she smiled. 'This one is for you.'

Miu purred with delight as the Pharaoh fastened the clasp. He silently thanked the goddess for helping him to find the Queen's necklace, and for protecting him as the Pharaoh's special palace cat.

The ancient Egyptians often included captions with their drawings, a bit like the words that go with the pictures in a comic. They explained what was going on in the pictures and sometimes gave the words which people were speaking.

The pictures in this book each have a caption hidden in them. The only problem is that they are written in hieroglyphs, the picture writing used by the ancient Egyptians. The Pharaoh in this story would have been able to read them… but can you?

See if you can spot the caption in each big picture. It should be easy to work out the ancient Egyptian word for cat because it is the sound a cat makes and is written with a picture of a cat.

The hieroglyphs actually say Miu, the word that was used for all cats as well as the name of the cat in the story. The first three pictures represent sounds, Mi then i then u or w. The last picture, of the cat itself, is called a determinative and is there to show exactly what the word means. Now you can use the guide below to work out what each caption says.

the cat hides

the cat leaps

44

the cat worships

the cat is miserable

the cat is praised by the king

Printed in Great Britain
by Amazon.co.uk, Ltd.,
Marston Gate.